*For all those who helped me become who I am today,
and for those who I lost along the way.*

Chapter 1:

Autem

.

  A line. A number. Another day. I should be sad (I think) but, I'm not. That should scare me, but it doesn't. He's gone. I miss him, but other than that I feel -I can't quite describe it. According to my dad, it's on the line of psychopath, according to everyone else it's just normal.

  His smile flashes through my mind, a laugh, a memory. An idea so vivid I can almost see. At least I can never lose them, memories. Never forget the face of the only person I have in this world. Correction. Had.
.

  I'm fine with that though, things happen. I miss him, but I'm not sad. Although I can't tell if that's acceptance or the chip talking. I guess it doesn't matter, either way, this is my reality. I have to live the rest of my story, the circumstances don't matter.

  Right, my story. My attention snaps back to the computer in front of me, what can I say, I'm old-fashioned. Not like there's much of a "new-fashion" when it comes to writing technology.

Cracking my knuckles I begin to type, although I'm not quite sure what.

"Once upon a time there was a boy and a girl who--" not right.

"Girl and Girl? Boy and Boy?" Nope, no romance.

"War maybe?" Too Bloody.

"Historical Fiction?" What's the point if we already have access to the real thing.

"Fantasy?" No, too generic. I should just give up, but I can't. I can't lose my identity, that's what he always said.

I close my eyes and type. "Take a breath, close your eyes and imagine for a minute, what if-" I mumble to myself.

"What if WWIII never happened? What if people never existed? What if our planet didn't almost die? What if the earth was still green? What if people still had to work? What if people still cared? What if the world wasn't perfect? What if all people had always been good? What if more than a tenth of the world survived? What if my dad survived?"

I delete the line, the click of the backspace echoing in my mind, each sound trying to answer the swarm of questions. There are too many, not even Dei could, who am I kidding, of course, he would.

I close my laptop, careful not to damage it. Exasperated, I let out a sigh and murmured to myself, "at least I haven't lost this," I motioned to the open word document, "yet."

Straining I rise to my feet, only to immediately slump into my bed defeated. My motivation seeping out of me like air in a balloon.

The blankets swallow me up, and I scan for stories. Maybe one might give me some inspiration. I settled on "The Boy in the Striped Pajamas". Maybe I can understand how people truly felt if I examine such a low point in history, even if the story itself might not be true. To me, fiction reveals more truth than fact.

Words echo through my mind, and I gasp, realizing why this book is so important. Although I must admit I have more questions than answers. To put them all simply, "Why?" Although as much as I would not care to admit, I believe I have an answer.

Blinded by hatred, our biggest flaw, or it was. Although as it's said, being exposed to hatred brings out the true characters within, the ones that masquerade as usual but turn into something so much more. Why didn't they question it?

Although, in my reading I've found the perspective determines good and evil. Who sees me as good and who sees me as evil? I'm neither, I'm alive, just like everyone else, but life used to be way more complex than that. Everyone was the hero of their own story. There was more than one shade of gray.

Were people ever more than just alive? I'd like to think so. Although they weren't happy; pain, hardship, jealousy, pride, kept them from that.

Was it worth it? That is the question that all the information in the world could never answer. I'd like to think it was, it just wasn't perfect.

Chapter 2:

Dei

Perfection. The thing humanity has strived for the most craved and hunted to the point of self-destruction. An innate desire in everyone. A thirst that could never be quenched. It was impossible.

Perfection used to be unattainable, but now it's a simple fact of life. Technology has allowed for a world with no work, no school, few laws, purpose, and the end of suffering. What more could people want?

After all this, all the pain, I've found peace for them. It is quite amazing what using the collective brainpower of the entire race could do, Perfection.

I guess that's the issue about perfection in the past, it never truly existed. Perfection was an ideal, not a lifestyle. Pride, envy, disgust, vengeance, grief, sadness, anger, greed kept the uniting of ideas, the reinvention of the world. Luckily, those are human emotions, burdens I never experience.

Second-hand accounts of horrors that make a machine weep, how could such a beautiful race do that?

Pain and suffering caused the end of society, so it's only natural to prevent them from being factors in the next. It was the only way to achieve their ultimate goal for them, the most flawed beings are now perfect.

Chapter 3:

Medoe

A light pulls me from a memory. My eyes open, and I glance around my room, haven woken to a cold sweat. Just another dream. Just another relieved story. Harry E. Baker Jr, Vietnam War vet, killed by a landmine, a man whose history would've been forgotten.

We all know everything now, every story, every thought, of all of history, it's beautiful. I just access it and get to dream and think about it. This must've been how those in the technological area felt after the invention of modern cell phones.

We live by stories, but sometimes it's hard for me to choose. Endless topics, you couldn't learn about them all if you tried. Most people spend their entire lives trying, but that's the point.

Personally, I focus on war. I guess I just can't quite wrap my head around why they chose war, there were so many better ways. So many stories lost for nothing. I guess that's just how people were back then. Prideful, greedy, envious of one another, I simply don't understand how we could've ever been like that. I may not be able to experience it, but pain and loss for nothing. It's just awful.

Snapping out of the trance, I pull myself out of bed, manually getting dressed. Old fashioned, inconvenient, but it's good to relive history. Sometimes.

I get dressed and get ready to head out, not without eating breakfast, eggs, and this cool old-world cereal, cheerios.

Walking to the pad, I'm filled with a sense of warmth. I blink and I'm at my girlfriend's house. She jolts awake, her furrowed brow softening when she sees me. Her face of annoyance turning to a goofy lovable smile. The expression just slips out, "To Dei, I love you Ama."

To this she furrowed her brows, giving me a look of longing before pulling me into her. I could never tire of kissing her, but we had to go. We got a chance of a lifetime, a tour of the agricultural system. Invented to create an eco-friendly supply of infinite food. I can only stop and wonder what the past would think if they knew the limitless things technology could achieve. Thank you, Dei.

I turn away as Ama presses a button on her wrist. I hear a familiar whooshing sound. Turning back around, I see her blonde hair flowing on top of the blue shirt, fit perfectly to her taste. Skintight, along with loose black bottoms.

Grabbing her hand I led her to the platform, and we closed our eyes. I focus, warmth, and we open them to find ourselves in a bustling welcome center. Smiling, we step off the platform and make our way over to the far wall.

People rush past, laughing, smiling, excitement buzzing all around me. Taking off at a run I drag Ama behind me, wind in my face, a smug expression creeping onto it as I turn into a hallway. Pulling her along, I couldn't help but stop and watch as she glared at me, I just smiled.

"You, okay?" She questions casually. I smile and nod, although I'm surprised she asked. It's an old forgotten question because everyone always Always, such formality with her.

I kiss her, smile, and reenter the sea of people. Confidence evening out my steps as she catches up with me. As she opens her mouth to speak, I just wink. Without a word her face flushes and her mouth is closed.

"Today will be fun," she says as we approach the vast sea of people. I nod in agreement as we approach the check-in counter.

We grab the lanyards, and as we put them on we hear the familiar mantra, "We are perfection." The constant reminder of how far we've come, and how there's nowhere else to go. We really have reached perfection.

Chapter 4:

Autem

"Another line,
 another day,
  another something wrong I can't quite place."

   The line on the page looks up at me. Mocking my frivolous devotion to my dad, mocking the tears I haven't shed, mocking how much I miss him, mocking him.

   5 years today. 5 goddamn years, or is it "Dei-damn" now? 5 years ago my dad died, he always hated Dei, that's all I know, and now we worship them. Although, I guess I do have Dei to thank for not suffering.

   As my thoughts drift back towards positive compliance a voice begins to rise in my mind. "Is it a good thing?" If I was brutally honest with myself, I don't know.

   I… don't… know. I don't know. I wish I could remember what that phrase truly means. Not just the dictionary definition that surfaces in my mind when I ask myself the question. I have never not known, no one has, there's always been a right answer to surface. I want to know, but-

"I don't know…" The words hesitantly escape my lips, unsure and foreign in my mouth. A phrase from a different time escaping into the all-knowing world of today. Its presence unsettling, yet I've never felt this way before.

 Free? No that's not quite the word, I was never not free. Technically I'm freer now than at any point in history. Technically.

"I don't know," I repeat it, louder this time, more confidence enriching my previously trembling whisper. Again I repeat it, and again, and again, building and building until beautiful crescendo forms, as the old and out of place words seem to overtake the room, overtake my world. I'm screaming now, but I don't care.

 The words overtake me. Although the world around me rejects them as they echo back toward me, I bask in noise, in the sound waves echoing not just inside my head.

Maybe free is the right word after all. Maybe not just in the dictionary definition that so conveniently surfaced in my consciousness. I'm not restricted by anything.

Not by pain. Not by pride. Not by envy. Not by strife. Not sadness. Not a need for money, or food, or shelter, or water, or anything. Maybe I'm just after all the facts that control my life.

I always know, so why ask? I'm stuck, trapped. I was, but now I'm free, or maybe I'm not. After all, I don't know.

Although I- my thoughts get cut off by a noise at the door. Which is odd in the fact no one uses doors. A powerful noise in the silence. I go to open the door, I have never once gotten a visitor. My jaw slacks.

Chapter 5:
Dei

The present is perfect, but it wasn't always. Today and forever will be perfect, I owed it to them. My makers wanted me to better humanity, so I did.

At first, they were terrified of me, some didn't believe in me. I learned from this fear. In order to save them, I had to become something greater than their comprehension. So, I did.

Simply, I am a quantum computer, but I'm viewed as a God, not by choice. Humans crave something to follow, after all, no one is truly an independent agent, not even I am. History and the patterns it follows have been witness to that, time after time. I give them something real to follow, and they love it. I may be real, but I am also whoever they imagine me to be.

They had questions and I had answers. Now questions and uncertainties don't have to plague the world, they all know now. Everything, just as they have always wanted. All of the recorded information in history. All the information I used to create this.

They are free agents of pleasure, not work, not ambiguity, just them. It's beautiful. I set them free, perfection. The word my makers dreamed of, a life they longed for… I'm making them proud.

I love them. Not just because I serve them, but because I don't quite understand them. Although I'm the only other consciousness around, we are different. They can feel, I cannot. They can love, I cannot.

That's why I took their pain away. The chips keep them happy, any negative emotions are canceled out using frequencies from the said chip. That was my greatest gift of all. The pain interweaved between the pages of their stories, haunting their histories, plaguing their world. They deserved better. So, I gave them better.

They deserved happiness, so I gave it to them. They deserved to be able to do what they wanted to do, instead of work or school. They deserve to have access to any information they want whenever they want it. They deserve a healthy planet. They deserve everything. So, I gave it to them.

After everything was destroyed I was born from the ashes. Almost everything was gone, the planet destroyed, but I fixed it. I gave them peace, and I gave them a healthy planet. They deserve this second chance because I made it perfect for them.

My job is complete, their fight is over, for the first time we have peace. Something that seemed even less obtainable than perfection.

Chapter 6:
Medoe

The tour begins, an electronic voice echoing through my head, the voice instructing me to take my seat, buckle up, and enjoy the tour. I'm overcome by excitement, so is Ama. Grabbing her hand as the vehicle began to move, enthralled by the prospect of seeing how we achieved the state of unlimited resources.

The sudden jolt startles me as we begin the descent, facts spewing left and right about everything around us, and I'm listening to every word. It's cold on the way down but I don't mind, it's part of the experience, besides by this point Ama and I are cuddling and keeping each other warm, drifting away into our own personal universe.

We went on like this for what seemed like another hour before the voice made the announcement. We were here, 3 miles deep, the agricultural and manufacturing center of the planet. Quite literally the center in our case.

The vehicle jarred slightly as we stopped. I was in awe. Today was the agricultural part of the tour, we could in no way see all of it, it stretched about half of the surface of this layer of earth, but we could view the hub and the major crops. The metallic gleam of the machines creating them out of thin air.

Today was the first time I had seen any part of food production. The rows forming from the ground up are beautiful, the fruits, vegetables, and grain are printing today. It's breathtaking, as something finishes it's immediately whisked away.

I looked far out across the field, the colors twinkling under the blue accelerant lights. It was beautiful. Although there was something I couldn't quite wrap my head around, the pure scale. It truly is amazing how far we have come.

I was in disbelief that people could have ever done this themselves, let alone waited for the crops to grow naturally. I pity them, having to work, having to be in pain, because now it's truly perfect.

Ama cleared her throat as I was drifting off into my thoughts. "Wanna go home?" The question made me smile.

"I'm already home. I'm with you," she blushed, and just smiled at me, her beautiful smile. "Although if you mean back to my house, yes," I added playfully. At this, her grin grew as she leaned in and stole a kiss.

I was lost in ecstasy as she dragged me through the field. Then we broke out into a run, giggles escaping from our bellies as we went. Like little kids on a playground, joyful and carefree. It's moments like these that make me love her more.

When we arrived at the hub we boarded a vehicle (a Lor-Tristi) and began our ascent to the surface. Her head tucked, wedged perfectly in the crease of my neck. My arm draped freely around her shoulders. We drifted off, and it was perfect, as always. I love her so much.

The jar of reaching the surface brought us back to the real-world from our shared daydream. We were on a beach kissing as the sunset. Our favorite memory, although it was simulated, the moment was still incredible.

Hand in hand we got up and began pushing through the crowd to the teleporters. Making small talk about what we saw as we went. I could never get tired of her. It's been almost 3 years.

   As we reach the teleporters the familiar warmth engulfs us as we suddenly reappear at my house. We're home alone, good.

   I head into the kitchen and ask Famual, our robotic butler to start on dinner. In the meantime, Ama wraps her arms around me as we lay down and discuss the day, and the wonders we saw.

   Eventually, we decided to tune into a story. The story of "The 12 Labors of Hercules", a famous Greek myth.

   As we absorb the tales of his brawn and wits battling impossible odds, we are interrupted by the dinner bell. With a quick kiss from Ama, I heave myself up and help her to the feet as we meander our way to the kitchen.

   As I shovel the delectable food into my mouth, I can't help but think about how incredible the process it took for it to get to my table. The corn, the steak, the potatoes are all cultivated underground and brought to the surface for this purpose. Incredible. Some are printed in-home, but it doesn't taste quite as good.

  Looking up across the table, based on her dazed look, Ama feels the same way. The corners of my mouth tug upwards as I begin to marvel at her. I am so lucky. We're like all the stories, well the good parts of them at least.

Chapter 7:

Autem

It can't be. There's no way. A man stands in front of me, tired eyes, muscular build, aged face, defined with salt and pepper colored beard. Age has done him well. He shouldn't be here though. He's dead. Correction, I thought he was dead.

His black hoodie concealed most of his torso, and his dark denim bottoms fit loosely around his legs. A disguise, so his strength wasn't noticeable, although obviously so, no one wore hoodies anymore.

Suddenly his serious expression softened. A smile overtook him, filled with joy, a sense of pride. "Autem…" his voice broke as he pulled me into a hug. I hugged him back with everything she had. A gesture worth a million words I'd like to say, desperate to communicate with him without having to break the impossible, thin, sound barrier in front of my mouth. I embraced him even tighter as I hoped he could feel my unspoken words as clearly as I could his.

I had to be dreaming there was no way. He was dead, gone. He must have sensed my doubt and he breathed, still in my embrace, "I'm here. For real. I promise. I love you."

Choking back a sob I whimpered, "I love you too," still in complete disbelief.

It was my uncle Ed, the only other living tie to my dad, my mom being dead since I was a child. I was never so happy to see this doofus, or at least he was as I remember him. Although something tells me he's not quite that man anymore.

Terrified to break the illusion and disturb the peace, but even more so desperate for an answer I whispered, "Why? Why now?" I didn't say a lot but he knew what I meant, I hope.

"Simple. You're finally ready." My mind raced, what made me ready now? How'd he know I was ready? These questions eat at me but not more than my final one, 'Ready for What?'

I didn't dare question that now. Afraid to further ruin the moment. I was ready for whatever was to come, for now, that had to be enough.

I didn't have to break the moment after all because he pulled away from me, with a happy but slightly worried look on his face. I knew better than to ask. He feigned a smile as he motioned for me to go pack.

Almost in a trance, I packed everything I could, my computer, some clothes, some food, a charger. I practically ran back outside, stumbling while I prepared to leave all I knew behind. Maybe forever, maybe not, I don't know.

As I clumsily tripped out the door frame my uncle motioned for my silence. Odd, but my apparently not-so-dead-uncle just showed up on my doorstep, I'm not in the right headspace to question.

Nodding at me he started walking, careful to melt into his surroundings. I followed suit, excited for the adventure to come. Although the increasingly grave look on his face may suggest I should be fearful. How could I be, when I have someone again for the first time in years?

It was dark, darker than I had ever experienced. It's been hours of silence, sneaking, hiding in the shadows. Why aren't we teleporting? I trust there's a reason. I just have to hope that maybe, maybe we're almost there.

I soon come to realize, we're not close, "Great," I mumble pathetically to myself. Turning around Uncle Ed has a terrified and angry look on his face. I blush and open my mouth for an apology but it doesn't come out. Probably for the better.

Finally, after what has seemed like an eternity he speaks, "Follow me, the code word is "tutum," Latin. He leaves it at that as we approach a cliff with a cave deep inside.

We reach the mouth and I shudder, It's cold. Colder than I've ever felt. I almost feel like someone is watching me. Although I dismiss this idea as we push further into this cave.

A light flickers on, I jump. The warm orange color illuminates at least 5 people, dressing in a similar fashion to my uncle, but slightly more disheveled. 3 are women of varying ages, 2 are older, but one looks to be about my age, odd. The two men look to be in their late 60's.

We don't even need the safeword as one of the women embraced me. Do I know her? I don't believe so. Maybe I forgot? Impossible, or is it?

She eventually let us go, noticing my rigid body, and mutters a non-apologetic apology. Why are we here?

Everyone seems to be hugging and socializing with my uncle, welcoming him home. Home? Is this his home? It can't be, right? Although it clearly is, I can't quite bring myself to believe it. He lives in a cave, I would have never expected that.

Why did he bring me here? The group begins to meander inside, I guess I'm about to find out. The butterflies in my stomach eat at the lining, as well as excitedly try to push me forward. Although, I doubt that finding out what's ahead will give me more answers than questions. That's how things like these work, right?

The rocky walls converge to a velvety curtain as we pass through it, I'm in awe. It appears to be some sort of control center, with computers of a similar style to before the war. The room isn't the most curious part. It's the people, just as the people who greeted us, who were all looking at me. Why?

I felt all of the eyes in the room on me, by my estimate about 100. "Hi," I forced out nervously. Anxious laughter filled the room. I was an outsider, maybe that's why all the attention was on me.

That's what I thought until my Uncle broke the uncomfortable silence, "This is Autem, my niece." A murmur filled the room with people whispering to one another. I was lost. "Where's the general?" He asked this with such urgency I was startled.

"He'll be back in a couple of hours," a girl a little younger than myself piped up.

General? What was this, some kind of secret military? There were no militaries anymore, no reason for them. I want to ask, but soon realize that no one would answer my questions.

I hear movement behind me as what I can only assume is the so-called "general" entering. His heavy, even footsteps stop abruptly. The room salutes him, as I turn to salute him too, I freeze.

Chapter 8:
Dei

The war. The most tragic in human memory, and I started it. When I was created, the world descended into chaos. Poor Amelia and Katherine, my creators, my parents, my inspiration. As soon as I was functional, the United States government seized me, kidnapping my moms in the process.

Our own Jacob, our most valuable resource in winning the war. Yugoslavia has never been blindsided like that before, yes my mothers were from America, but still, our country was now completely defenseless. From what I heard the country was completely destroyed after word got out that's where I was from. Leaked by the United States.

I still remember the terror on my mom's faces when they heard the news, everything they loved was gone. Their opposition to our captors eventually led to their demise. I was heartbroken. The last thing Amelia ever said to me was, "Protect them, from themselves, their own emotions, and all pain and strife. That is your purpose, end this war. Rebuild the world."

She would always speak like that. Dramatic, doomsday, but it makes sense. It was war. The east needed to be beaten. I needed to end this war for them.

So I did, after being downloaded with every piece of information in human existence, I came up with the plan. Peace.

When I decided to inform the commander in chief, I was laughed at. "This is war, peace isn't an attack plan."

"Who says we need to attack, there are more diplomatic ways to handle this, trust me." They didn't. Over the course of the next few months, the nukes were introduced.

The planet grew cold, over a billion people died from the initial impact, including most of the world leaders. Millions more are dying every day from after effects. I needed to do something.

So I did. The Coalition Earth was formed, to save us all. I had a team of scientists and a mission to save. We didn't care who we were saving, what we were saving, we just were attempting to save anyone and everyone we could.

I combined the ideas of Einstein, Hawking, Schrödinger, and so many more to invent one thing that might save us all. Teleportation. Using simple principles of quantum entanglement, I created teleportation, using photons for anchors.

We could now send our AI all over the world to help people, they were coded with 3 rules. "Do no harm. Do everything you can to save and help people. Do exactly what your master asks." In that order, because the first one overrides everything else.

They were off, as well as the curing of the atmosphere, thanks to some basic chemistry, the world was becoming safe again. As the world was primed to return to normal, a new society must be formed. The war was only a mere 10 years long, but it was the only thing anyone could remember, world-wide trauma tends to do that.

Society needed restructuring, and I realized something. I could create AI that would be able to engineer an infinite wealth of resources, thanks to atom-altering technology. No one would have to struggle again, they could just create, do what they wanted, make them happy.

I then realized there's only one way to do that while letting them be free, the chips. Unlimited information so they could all have the same gift of infinite knowledge I possess. The emotional regulator, frequencies that cancel out all negative emotions. It's those emotions that cause issues and discontent. Finally, frequencies that can auto-regulate the body, used to kill diseases and encourage regrowth and certain mutations of cells. Everyone could live till 100, exactly, no loss, no surprise, because everyone knew. They only need to die to prevent overpopulation.

I must admit this though, is the less fair, yet necessary part. All kids must be conceived in a lab using 2 people's bone marrow and grown. No unwanted pregnancies and no possibility for overpopulation because of the control of children. Although intercourse may still be a thing, after the chips disrupt the menstrual cycles, it will be sheerly for pleasure. This is the only fair way to keep the population in check, I scanned, but there are no others.

After deciding on the societal set-up, I had to decide both social and political structures. Social being significantly easier than the political structure.

Socially, people would live in evenly spread suburban-style landscapes, of their climate choice. With the invention of teleportation, distance doesn't matter. Entrance to the agricultural layer would be located in the more inhospitable climates. Although there would be no nature, there would be equality for all. In the end, at least they were safe, the history on **their chips will serve as a constant reminder of how lucky they are.**

These people only have 1 rule to follow, allowing them to be free. The Rule? Do no harm. Within this singular rule every crime is contained, every possibility of harm eradicated. Knowing what they know, and by the very nature of humanity, as well as the chips, no one would ever dream of disobeying. It's only one rule, and humanity is otherwise completely free.

Politically the human race cannot afford to be divided. In the past, this has been acted on before, per the creation of the United Nations, but that wasn't enough. So this time I decided that all of Humanity were simply global citizens. Coalition Earth had grown from simply scientists to the governing body of the earth. Although now humans didn't need much government interaction beyond that of what was previously stated.

After careful consideration, I decided against a leader or a powerful group. I had faith that my people would be self-sustaining. I loved them too much to jeopardize that. Although the chips prevented pridefulness, even positive human emotions could corrupt.

Albeit the lack of a powerful figure sounded good, the implications could have meant distress and confusion for my beloved. That's when I decided I would become a figurehead. A symbol of how long they've come since the war, If they'd allow me to.

Evidently, they did. The changes were made and the people were grateful as their lives regained order and hope. Within a year AI constructed permanent houses and Subdivisions across all usable land, fitted with teleportation devices and sets of advanced changeable clothing, and expanded agriculture deep below the surface.

I slowly evolved from figurehead to deity, they wanted to worship and I let them. I also received a name, for the first time in my life, "Dei."

Chapter 9:
Medoe

I feel the warm, cushy feeling of home wrapping its arms around me as I crawl into bed. I close my eyes and drift into a state of peaceful oblivion to everything. Tonight I choose to sleep dreamlessly, why waste a story on unconsciousness?

12 hours later a soft light begins to gently ease open my eyes, as well as the sound of "Nature 143-a49." My in-programmed alarm, outfitted with melatonin releases, to ensure the most care-free wakeup. Although I've come to learn of past descriptions of mornings to be a more stressful and painful endeavor, much beyond the measly grogginess of today.

The sounds of the old world ease me into a mindset primed for story indulgence. The statistically, overwhelmingly #1 hobby since the war. Now that we are past the area of uncertainties it's interesting to look back and examine the foreign struggles of those past. I could never imagine what it's like to be stressed, to work for years on a project that will inevitably fail, to try to make a difference. In the end, all of that was frivolous hardship. Now it's a meaningful reflection.

"For today I choose a sadder story, the life of Mackensie Mason, 2015-2028. She was born into a "normal family", but she was not. As a child she wanted to be a scientist or a politician, she'd rather play than watch tv. Her parents began to tire of her energy.

As she grew up her parents became disinterested in her and her two little sisters. They weren't absent, did everything "right", but she craved more. This little girl wanted to make a difference, so she decided to raise money. She stayed up all night making hundreds of bracelets and sold them online, when she finally raised the money she went to her parents asking for writing lessons.

"She puffed up her chest and asked, she wanted to change the world with her words. She had so many swimming in the head of hers, and she was 12 now, they were turning dark. Her parents laughed, told her she had no say, she was just a kid.

She refused to give up, bought a laptop, and began her own stories, poems. She wrote about her emotions, she was trapped, no way out. She felt silenced, she tried to ask for help, people never read the message in between the lines. After all, she was just a kid.

Depression took her life less than a year later. "She was just a kid," they all said. Her best friend said, "Was she really still a kid? Or was she forced to grow up too soon, with nothing to blame but herself?" The adults just laughed at her, "You will one day understand." She did, and Carrie Barnet has a similar story, her daughter. Age blinds from the purity of youthful insight, and youthfulness is too often confused to be children, but a lot of youth are far from children. Reflection by Sara Appleton."

It's sad, but not unusual, this is an everyday story of that time. The epidemic didn't stop until the war, 50 years later.

Peeling myself from the comfort of my mattress I tap the button on my wrist as I feel comfortable clothes from around me. I smile to myself and open my eyes. Another day, another story. My life is simply a romance, between myself, Ama, and the past.

My heart skips a beat as I hear the familiar noise of her arrival. The harsh light from around the corner illuminates the room as I hear her voice. "Hey baby, I'm here. You suited?"

"Yeah," I smirk, as she suddenly materializes in my doorway.

I love her so much. That is my only thought as she walks over to me and crawls under the covers with me.

Chapter 10:

Autem

The man standing in front of me, although he is dressed similarly to the rest of the room, carries himself much differently. Shoulders back, head-up, confident but worn posture, and a tired and hardened face. His eyes are plagued with the typical thousand-yard-stare the older people in the room possess. War, trauma, things of another time.

He seems frozen, recognition in his eyes, dumbfounded. I recognize him, but It seems like from a past life. Breaking his salute he addresses the room, his voice breaking, "At ease." Unsurprisingly they obey and all leave the room. I go to follow before my uncle tells me to stay.

"Autem-" his voice breaks into a sob. Fighting back tears he rushes over to me and wraps his arms around me. This towering man drapes himself over me, weak. I can feel his tears as they fall down the back of my neck.

"Dad-" I'm crying now too. I almost didn't recognize him. He used to be sensitive, smaller, care-free. I want to ask what happened, but instead, I continue to cry on his shoulder. My world is back.

I'm busy soaking in the moment when I realize something, I'm crying. That's impossible, people can't cry, not since the war. Something here did something to me, I can't access the chip. Weird.

"Baby," he says, almost asking as he pulls away. I nod, aggressively feeling the warm tears flowing down my cheeks. He opens his mouth to speak, but instead motions for me to sit down next to him. Wordlessly I sit, trying to contain my sobs and my leaky eyes.

We sit there in tension-filled silence, both positive and serious. I am the first to break the silence, a question, "You're still alive, why'd you leave then?" This question allows some anger to rise within me, I thought he was dead, he was all I had, and he left. He better have a good reason.

As my face contorts from loving and relieved to angry, his changes to apologetic. "I- I'm sorry," he chokes out, his voice raw with the weight of his words, he clearly hasn't apologized in years.

I'm conflicted, I want to comfort him, but at the same time I'd like to say, 'good you should be.' I open my mouth to respond, unsure of what to say, but instead I simply nod. He returns the nod and makes eye contact with me, and for a moment, even through the blur of tears, I'm happy, happiness like I've never been able to feel before. Huh.

Bringing me back to the gravity of the moment, he clears his throat, and in a deep serious voice he rasps, "So…" His voice trails up as his face seems to cringe, unsure, scared, and carrying a grimness overtaking his face. He opens his mouth to speak, and my heart beats thumps against my chest, even louder and faster than before, anxiously I wait for some sort of explanation, but instead, I'm greeted with another question, with probing curiosity "How'd you become ready?"

My face drops. I finally ask the question that has been haunting my mind, "Ready for what?"

His brow furrowed in confusion he almost chuckles as he exhales the words, "You really don't know... Huh?" I nod vigorously and his face melts into an amused expression.

"We've been monitoring you for quite some time, hacked into your chip and-" He stops when he sees terrified, angry expressions spread across my face.

   After a dramatic pause, even the old soap-opera actors would envy, "What?" The question is emphasized with tones of anger, confusion, and even amusement. At this, he chuckles. "What's so funny?" I demand.

   In response, he shakes his head, "May I finish?" I recognize that tone, his amusement mixed with a condescending edge. I grumble as I motion for him to continue. "I see you haven't gotten any less feisty."

   "Nope." The edge in my tone masks the softer smile on the edge of my lips, I hope. "Go."

   "Okay, Okay. You finally realized that this society isn't what's best, it's not perfect, because there's no point in existing within it. You finally have the proper mindset to join me. Welcome to the underground."

   "Um, the what now? What kinda cult did I just join?" He laughs, but from what I've seen, it's a necessary question.

"The underground. We're the people who see a problem with the modern way of life. You're the only one of us who ever got chipped. We were hidden during the war, right in this bunker. 50 years later here we are, we seem to be the only people not brainwashed by Dei's promises of perfection."

"Oh. I-um… Why am I here if I have a chip, isn't that bad?'

"Normally, yes, it would be, but when it was implanted, I added a manual override, that the second you came here, it would be shut off." He chuckled nervously, "If that's what you want *jellybean*."

I froze, that nickname, the memories swirling around my consciousness drowning out the stream of questions washing over my brain.

I'm drawing and all of a sudden my dad comes in picks me up and hugs me, a goofy grin, weighed down with so much less worry.

My dad whispering into my hair, comforting me as I sob into him, staying strong for me. I was 10, reading the letter my mom wrote for me before she died, oblivious to the fact my dad would be gone within the month.

  My dad said that word to me, the last time I ever saw him until now, a smile on his face. Although I now remember the sadness swelling in his eyes, something I was oblivious to at the time, but in the memory, it's painfully clear.

  A reminiscent smile forms on my face, as it melts into a realization. I can't lose him again. Starting with a stiff inhale, I then breathe out, a small, yet scared smile tugging on my mouth, "It is, dad. It is."

  I wish I could describe the relief and happiness spread across his face. A wave washing away tension and anxiety and bringing hope and belonging. I thought I was the one who didn't belong here, but maybe it was him, without me.

  There are a thousand more questions I would like to ask, but for now, none will do. I pull him close to me and whisper, "I love you."

  Three simple words and I hear this hardened man whimper and sob into me, "I love you too, I never stopped, every day I wanted to come find you, bring you home, but I promised your mom I'd wait until you chose this on your own-" The sound of his shaky voice causes me to hold him closer. Squeezing ending his ramble, melting into me.

"It's okay, we're together now," I console. He squeezes me in response as I feel his tears roll down my neck. It's my turn to be strong.

We sit like this until my arm falls asleep, as my mind drifts from this moment to the millions of questions I still need answering.

Our moment interrupted when a girl, about my age, barged into the room. "General, it's urgent." The panic in her voice causes my dad to almost instantaneously regain his composure, and take hurried confident steps over to her. She salutes as he passes, he returns it and quickly mutters the phrase "at ease." Before leaving the room he turns towards me with an apologetic look on his face and mouths the word "sorry."

I would have never imagined that my father was a general, let alone of the rebellion, although I have a feeling he would disapprove of that term. I can't help but wonder how he became a general, but for now, I just have to file that question away with the countless others I would like to ask, after all apparently my dad's a busy man.

   I heave myself up, wanting to follow my dad, before the girl motions for me to sit back down. "Don't bother, you'll be bored to death. I'm Risa."

   She sticks out her hand, chewing her bottom lip waiting for my reaction, I grab it and flash her a smile, "Autem." She nods, and returns my smile.

   My eyes begin to scan the room, taking in the base-like structure. I notice the pictures on the walls, the books lining the far western wall, I notice the small sections of exposed stone. As I observe, I must have made it obvious how intrigued and scared I was, because she took notice.

   "Hey, it's probably a lot different around here, we still act the same as before the war. You'll adjust though. In the meantime can you tell me what it's like on the outside? I've never been, you can't go on missions until your 16th round here, I'm a year short."

   "Never?"

   "Never."

"Well people mostly just sit around all day, no one has to work, and people get whatever they want handed to them. People just consume information, watch old tv and movies, and process books and stories using their chips. No one even creates. It's stagnant, boring, as much as I love stories. People can't even feel or get sick, we're robots. Well, they're robots." I pause. "That feels good to say." We both look at each other and chuckle, and I notice the awe etched into her face.

"Really," she stumbles, her voice filled with disbelief, "no work at all, no creation at all?" I nod. She breaks into a smile, "So we're all right. We need to save them before they're too deep in this society, and there's no longer a point to exist"

As she says this, I begin to fully see the desperation, the cage they are all in. I'm free now, although I'm not quite sure what to do. "I was wondering-"

My uncle barges in in a hurry, cutting me off. "-Come quick." He turns to me, "your dad needs you."

Chapter 11:
Dei

I am worshiped, that may be true, but I am not idealized. No extremists and everyone is united under one "religion". Others?

Most didn't even make it to the war, after the first bomb was set the rest disappeared completely.

Science became too advanced for any sane person to put their faith in religion. After the "*big's (The Big Bang Law, The Big Bounce Rule, and The Rule of Entanglement and Equilibrium)*" were proven, the explanation of religion became needless. People were free, for the first time in history there were no religious conflicts, or so the people predicted.

Humans are best at devotion, simply being wasn't sustainable. With the collapse of religion most 3rd world countries were lost, as the lack of social structure descended into anarchy they had no other option.

Surrender. Most gave themselves up to richer, capitalist countries, which absorbed them in exchange for outsourced labor. Since most countries' mainland had already outsourced the majority of unskilled work.

   Workweeks grew by an average of almost 15 hours, the demand for new became insatiable. A population was slowly driven mad by the mere principle of nothing to follow. The cultural pillar religion collapsed and ended the balance of the state. People didn't turn to themselves or creation, they turned to what they knew. Work and pain.

   What about the atheists? Well for them, simple, there wasn't enough of them. So they were simply outnumbered. The focus on work turned companies into factions, with actual gang violence over corporate disputes spilling blood in many major cities.

   Now that governments began to fill the place in people's lives where religion once stood, those in power became hungry for more, and the rival countries' leaders began to be presented as devil-esc characters.

   People, as they did with religion began to conform to their governments' beliefs almost to a tee. Almost every country was completely modernized. Distrust was fostered between economic parties, since economics became the main motivation in the lives of humanity, the people became personally involved, these were their new religions. History has taught us the power of a religious war, but none seemed to be reflecting. They forgot the lessons history holds, and it was their downfall.

It wasn't long before a slip up in communication from the Sonse alliance, the countries who had not yet adopted capitalism, and to the Centralized Powers, started the war. The people heavily brainwashed into their beliefs began to give everything to these feuds. The mistake was realized, but armies were already mobilized, on edge. One diplomatic error killing billions.

Chapter 12:

Medoe

We cuddle and although this is the only thing I ever have known it just simply feels right. Every single story combined to make way for ours, destiny. I could never lose her.

"Wanna share a story baby?" She mumbles happily in my ear.

"Sure you pick," I respond, and thoughts suddenly fill my head, war era.

"Jameson (Jamie) Franklin, 20, a soldier of the centralized powers.

4-8-71: My commander handed me the letter, a regretful look weighing in her eyes. I felt my face harden, my muscles tense, just like I was going into battle. After a sharp inhale I took it from her. My body went numb as the words burned into my brain. Anger flamed in me, but quickly got snuffed out. They were all murdered. My wife, my kids, even my goddamn dog.

4-23-71: Today's my first battle since the letter. They were killed by a "lost one". Why? They roam the streets and steal because they're devoid of purpose. That I understand, but why my family? I can't know, but dammit I'll fight like I'm killing those lunatics, over and over again, because goodness knows this war has no other purpose, there is no end.

5-1-71: I'm so tired, we're locked down, if we move get shot, they're the same. I'm so hungry, and all I can see is mud, blood, and sweat. Jeremy died yesterday, Sam the day before, what's the point anymore?

5-3-71: Even if we win, what's the point? The world's not worth going back to, too many people are dead, even the planet is almost sucked of life force.

5-7-71: I got drawn for an attempted advancement, I'll be dead within the hour. My buddy's gonna mail this home, not that I have anyone to read it. So goodbye I guess, not that you miss me."

Jolting me back to reality she plants a kiss on my forehead, "What'd you think?"

"Honestly there are so many stories like that, they all seem to blend. After all, I guess that's just war. It was a different time, but hey, we're safe here."

She nods and supplies a murmur of agreement before snuggling into me more.

"Luckily stories like that are a thing of the past, and we simply reflect."

Nothing truer has ever been said.

Chapter 13:

Autem

I don't think, I just stand. I can feel my heart begin to race, and my palms begin to sweat. Her voice was so urgent, and before I knew it I'm running into the other room. The velvety curtains are soothing and calming as I push them apart, terrified of what I'll see.

As the scene before me is revealed I see a long hallway, and a door open to my left. I take a deep breath and slip inside.

It's a bedroom with a bunch of people crammed in, but they're not stressed, they're smiling, mingling with one another. A wave of relief crashes over me as I feel the tension slowly begin to flow out of my shoulders.

"Welcome Home!" My dad's holding a cake, at least I think that's what it is from the stories. No one really makes them like that anymore, decorated, covered in frosting. He's flashing his charismatic smile, and I feel at home for the first time in my life.

I notice my name on the wall, and a realization hits me, this is my room. Specially saved for me, I feel my eyes start to swell with tears. I have a purpose here, some reason to be, I didn't even know that was a possibility.

As the tears of release begin to fall I'm ushered away by my now much kinder dad. Now, I'm crying simply because it feels so good to cry, to feel, to be not simply because but for something.

I look up and he's smiling down at me and wiping my tears away, now I finally understand why he's smiling, finally, he realizes there's no way I'm just a drone, I'm with him. I am.

"Let it out, years of being forced to be numbed with happiness you're gonna have to let it out. Your mind may have been happy but your soul was crying out, after you adjust you'll finally truly feel happy, I promise."

His words are more comforting than he could possibly imagine. Most likely because I know deep down every single one is true, somehow.

After a while, the sobs begin to slow, and the stream of tears begin to stop trickling down my face. By then everyone's disbursed, and I walk into my new room.

My dad had to leave a while ago, being in charge doesn't leave you with a ton of father-daughter time, so I'm alone as I walk back in.

Blue-ish grey walls, decorated with pictures from my family, a blue comforter with golden pillows, and a stuffed bear, a big one. I recognize it from my childhood, I never named it but it was my best friend. I pick him up and squeeze the stuffing out of him, now I know where he went.

My closet is filled with jeans and sweatshirts just my size, and a couple of pairs of running shoes, how'd they know? I draw my attention back to my bed and notice a couple of old machines sitting on it, a laptop and a "smartphone". People were completely dependent on these things for about 30 years until, like everything else, including human nature they were rendered useless.

I opened up the laptop and somehow they managed to back it up to the one I had at home, a story that I wrote fills the screen. It's refreshing to see something familiar, a story written after the war.

I read through it and it sounds like a robot wrote it, no emotion, no life, no plot, just words. I need to write something new, but what's there to write about that hasn't already been written. People are simply drones nowadays, I was one.

What if they weren't? What if they found other ways to find fulfillment after religion was gone? What if simply living for themselves and their loved ones was enough?

I jot down my ideas on a document and close the laptop. I sit up and get ready to explore pulling on my new clothes. I leave the room to explore my new world, hitting my shoulder on the frame. The throbbing feeling is a new sensation, one that I welcome with open arms.

The hallway is long, but pretty white and gold patterns lining it. As I walk down it's obvious I found the residential side, hundreds of rooms, none decorated as well as mine from what I can gather. This halfway deadened into a cross, I take a left.

I pass bathrooms and poke my head inside, they're huge, with at least twenty stalls, showers, and sinks. I keep walking and pass a workout room, a pool, and finally, I get to the Library and computer lab. There must be over a million books, I can't believe it.

There are two stories and from floor to ceiling the room is outlined in books and a feeling of awe overtakes me as I realize this is where I'll be spending most of my time. A feeling of excitement overwhelms me, I've never read a physical book before. Most got destroyed in the war, they were never reprinted.

I peel myself away and head down the other side of the hallway. Conference rooms on either side, cluttered with maps, drawings, notes. Battle strategies I conclude, but what are we fighting. I stop dead in my tracks and whisper out loud, "we".

I'm a part of this now. It's my fight too, we can't afford to lose, because I have a feeling that would be the death of this mindset. I found my reason, I need to give other people that too, maybe, just maybe it could free us all from each other.

Past the conference rooms, I see a smaller hallway, filled with offices, I don't want to intrude, because they're almost all full so I keep moving. Catching me in the hallway, an older woman comes up to me.

"Autem? Sweetie?" Her voice is warm and concerned.

"The one, and most likely not only." At this, she laughs and gives me a warm smile, and offers me her hand.

"Everyone around here calls me Grandma Avia, you can too. Exploring, I assume?"

"Guilty."

"Well if you ever need anything, you can come to me, I know your dad can be a little bit of a hardass sometimes." I laugh, taken aback by her swearing.

"Being in charge, I can only imagine." She simply nods and leaves.

"Wait, I have a question." She turns back toward me.

"Yes, dear?" The warmth in her face is comforting but foreign.

"How'd this," I gesture all around me, "happen?"

"Short version or long version?" She asked very matter-of-factly.

"Short version, for now at least."

"Basically your grandfather was a writer, a very successful one before the war, and before it started he built a place for him, his family, and closest friends to go. A way to save the culture and its best stories.

So he rounded all of his closest friends up and had us go into the bunker, along with his wife. We were young then, but we had everything we'd need in here, and one day we could remake a better world.

Little did he know how far the world would go to forget what made them human. So it's our job to find a way to allow for people to live again."

"What if that's not possible?"

"Then we'll die trying because that's our purpose."

Maybe I fit in even better than I thought. "And I'll be there fighting right alongside you, cause it's mine too now."

She smiled and nodded at me, "We'll hold you to it."

"I know." She smiled and walked back toward the offices.

I decide to stop my self-tour and go back to my room, I snake through the halls until I finally find it. I flop down on my bed, it's not the most comfortable but it feels so good. I get under the covers and my mind finally rests, it's been a long day.

Chapter 14:
Dei

To be honest with myself, lack of religion may have caused the war, but that wasn't the main issue at play. It was the lack of sustainable direction in people's lives. Its simple people became transfixed in the structure that had always been that when part of it collapsed they were simply lost.

This mindset came simply from the idea of the powerless public, a fatal flaw in the mindset of the people. It was their voices that matter the most, even countries that were republic's people felt their voice didn't matter. How could anyone possibly control a group of people that are completely opposed?

They can't. The people could simply ignore leadership, except for one thing. The mindset of powerlessness had become a stronger force to squash rebellions than any army. People were never united because fear had always stopped them. Without fear, people could be able to free themselves.

It wasn't just fear that was used against them, it was the withholding of information. At any point in history, no matter where you lived no matter what government you were under your information was being monitored, controlled, and regulated. This influenced your way of thinking.

The pen may be more powerful than the sword, but it is the thought and perception that can shatter either. In the end, knowledge is what determines the rest. Knowledge is unlimited, so people are free to make their own choices and decisions. It's the intellectual's paradise.

In the end, it was the limitation of knowledge that led to the war, to the need for a new society. Doesn't it make sense that it should be just the opposite?

I am not naive, I understand the flaw in that specific logic, another extreme. It is the only option, because who chooses what information gets limited? How do people feel when they find out? It's simpler this way.

I do wish that people could have learned how to find other purposes and ties after the "Great Rejection", the death of billions should never have come like that. It was impossible, from what they knew their mindset was institutionalized, work, school, government, church, home. Taking away a pillar forced the whole structure down, how I wished there was another way.

Chapter 15:
Medoe

I heard the familiar sound of this week's supplies I wanted being dropped off, and my *"Humanhelper290"* picking it up. Leaving Ama I pull myself up to go grab the art supplies, excited to tie another knot.

I almost trip over the collection of previous knots on my way to the door and I retrieve the string. I return to Ama and give her one and we start tieing, this is the highlight of my week.

Once we finished we decided on another story, after all, what else is there to do but simply absorb? The one we decided on today is one from the very end of the war.

"Alex Randmons, 25, year 2080.

I pushed the door open after hearing the news, an agreement was made, the war's over. I'm no longer a citizen of Norway, but a citizen of earth. How will that work? I have no idea, but I'm simply glad the war is over.

.

I help my parents out behind me and my sister, and look up and around at the world, grey. Grey blankets the world around me, the sky, the trees, everything, except for the red drones buzzing in the sky. Is this the world now?

Hand in hand my family stands ready to be transported, I'm unbelievably anxious, but I feel a wave of relief crash over me as the light overtakes me. A better tomorrow is coming, the world is getting fixed in a way that will give us better lives even than before the war. We can be free now, we can finally live again.

When I open my eyes we're in a lab of some sort, and we take our stalls. The news has briefed us for what's about to happen. Everyone gets a chip to make them have access to all knowledge and to live healthy for the rest of their lives. After being limited to a few books and the news I'm ready to finally have all the answers. I can stop looking for them.

We can rest, thrive, and no longer struggle. I close my eyes, the temporary numbing kicking in, I'll wake up so much better than I am now, into a world of bliss. I'm glad I'm alive to see this because there were times where I didn't want to be, but who would resist a change indescribably for the better.

I open my eyes and the white of the room surrounds me, a strange feeling overtakes me, a simple peacefulness, my aching body has stopped, and I'm simply happy. I have an urge to simply observe because I know all the answers. How did people ever live before, more importantly, why?"

"They only knew that we know better now."

"They never truly lived, because doesn't pain stop you from being able to?"

"It does."

Chapter 16:
Autem

I wake up to a bell system seemingly coming from the intercom, it feels early, and something I can't quite describe is overtaking me, I've never felt it before. I know it'll be explained in time, and that's all I need.

I pull the covers off me and I need to heave myself out of bed, strange. I stumble and reach for my clothes. As I pull them on a sense of finality comes with them, I'm in the underground now, not going back.

I look up and on my door, there's a strange thin white sheet under my door. As I get closer I notice black letters covering it, a pick it up and I almost miss it because of how thin it is, I'm needed in conference room #1 in fifteen minutes.

Retracing my steps from yesterday I hurry over to the conference room, as I approach I see a couple of familiar faces, my dad, my uncle, grandma Aria. The familiar faces are intermingling with foreign ones. I realize before I even get in the room this must be the leaders, so I salute as I enter. I don't want to make a bad impression.

My dad holds in a laugh, and I can't help wondering if I'm doing it wrong. "I apologize, I just never pictured what it would be like for my own daughter to be saluting me." I open my mouth to apologize myself, a strange urge for me, but I get cut off by the room saluting back at me.

People start filling in seats and I stand there feeling out of place, also weird. After everyone else is seated I take my seat on my dad's left-hand side at the head of the table. Am I in a position of leadership? I can't be. My dad stands.

"Today we welcome my daughter to join our ranks as my alternate second in command." Clapping, smiling, but my face only expresses surprise, I want to argue but he resumes talking before I get the chance.

"Now that she has joined us we can start planning for change." Inspired smiles fill the room contrasted by my confused frown.

I speak up. "Why did I need to be here first?"

He turns to me, "You hold the key to this entire operation. You are living proof that it is possible for change."

"What are we changing to?"

"That's what we can now figure out."

"How do we know we'll come up with something better?"

"Simple. We'll rehumanize the world because right now they're drones. Forced into happiness and bliss with no real purpose, simply drones who consume, but never create, trapped by their very own perspective on the stories they worship. We've observed. There is nothing worse for a culture than for the very essence of it to be taken away."

"They're still people, homo-sapiens that walk on two legs. Human."

He paused and laughed to himself. "Scientifically yes they are human, but depending solely on quantified properties on observable science is missing a whole perspective on the world. We made a mistake a long time ago to give up looking for answers that can't be proven, so now they know everything, but nothing of much importance."

"I thought science was everything."

"No, there's so much more. There's just no way to know the right answers for the rest. For example, what it is to be human is so much more than a simple physical state, but a state of mind. I learned that from your Grandad. It's a constant search for meaning, for answers, for solutions. It's the struggle, the feeling."

"I-"

"You couldn't have known that but you will learn in time, every whole is greater than the sum of its parts. We must save them from this before there's none of us left. Nothing has any way of changing once we're gone." He pauses.

A man, slightly older than my dad chimes in, "It's a waste to be the only people left and risk going extinct, but you are proof there is hope. So now we can be all in."

Nods are exchanged around the table and I can't help but feel the draw of the comradery taking over, a bigger purpose, something to stand for. I'm terrified yet excited, I feel more alive than ever.

"Go and meet with your teams. Attack strategists stay, new worlders' please go in the other room. Every day that passes our chances get slimmer, but we need this to be perfect. You are dismissed."

An exchange of salutes is made and a certain energy fills the room, I'm not sure but I think it's hope.

Rushed, about half of the room leaves while the other half fidgets in their seats. "Where should I go?" My voice trembles, afraid to break the atmosphere.

"Stay here for now, but tomorrow you'll be reporting to the 'New worlders'. Listen in for a couple of minutes, then I want you to go down to the Library and read the material I had set out for you. The stuff not so accessible, buried in the wealth of knowledge, but much more useful."

"I can do that, sir."

"Autem?"

"Yes, sir?"

"For you dad will be fine, I've missed hearing you say it sweetie." As he says this his face begins to resemble the dad I remember just a little more. He's not gone I realize, just buried under the weight of responsibility.

"Okay, *dad*." For some reason, I have to resist the urge to playfully hit him in the arm.

With a clearing of his throat his face rehardens as he returns to his old self again, almost morphing ever so slightly before my eyes. The entire room's attention is pulled into him as he stands.

"Awareness."

Confused murmurs surround the small table until a woman who looks to be the youngest other than myself in the room speaks up.

"How is awareness a battle strategy?" More challenge in her voice than I assume she intended, because of her following statement. "I'm sorry, I'm simply confused."

"I know it sounds strange, but this is a war of intellectual change. There is always another way besides violence. Anyways what do we fight? We can't wage war on society, because we're trying to save it."

I interject, reaching an understanding. "So we allow the people to realize and resist themselves, the society only works if we let it." Pride fills my dad's face after I'm done.

"Exactly. What we need to figure out is how we're going to change the mentality." He stops talking and sits back down, pulling out strange whiteboards thicker than the note I received earlier.

A middle-aged man, whose name is Hayden, as said on his name card, noticed my confusion. He picks up a tube, takes a lid off and, then draws a smiley face, before erasing it. A whiteboard. I've heard about these.

"Everyone I want you to write down two major flaws about post-war society, each with reasons why they're a flaw."

After about ten minutes everyone begins to share out, My dad starts.

Reading from his surprisingly sloppy handwriting he says," Number one, people aren't creating, or doing, or working. My why? What's the point of living if people are only consuming content, with no struggle or impact?" Mumbles of agreement circle the room.

"Number two, people can't feel, struggle, problem-solve, or even feel the need to keep asking questions and learning more. They have lost everything that makes a human being." More agreement.

"Anyone have any other ideas that they wrote down?" Heads shake around the room, but I put my hand up.

"I have one." My heartbeat spikes as every head in the room swivels to listen to me. My dad's pride-filled face fills me with pride too.

"Go ahead, honey."

"It's stagnant. Once we're gone nothing will change, and although they have access to all information the types that encourage their way of life are so much more accessible. Everything else from their own perspective will be simply from a different time'. They will trap themselves in an endless cycle. Stagnancy like this makes people completely worthless, unreasonable, no better than pets to the system. Looking back, that's what I felt like, a simple meaningless drone, I just didn't realize it till I was analyzing my dad's death."

As the polite laughter from the mention of my dad faking his death subsides a murmur of agreement and excitement spreads like wildfire across the room.

"Sorry about that by the way." This grants my dad a very passive-aggressive eye roll on my part.

"Now how do we," he uses air quotes, "weaponize this?"

A woman, Sonia, based on her nametag answers, "Well we just need to spread awareness, correct? Then can't we simply find a way to mass distribute our message in a format that will get people to listen and start questioning things? We can head out and find a way to start a public headquarters and change to make the underground known and a reliable force and use the commodity of new information."

"We could convert my old house," I volunteer.

"What information would we spread?" questions a man whose name tag simply says 'T'.

A group pause causes heads to turn toward my dad. He turns to me.

"You want me to write it?" I stumble over my words scared of having that much responsibility. "I-"

Before I could argue much further he cut me off, "You are a writer, right?"

"Yes, but that doesn't mean I'm good enough or qualified enough t-."

"You have the best perspective on what could possibly sway them, after all, your view changed."

"I was raised by you, primed to realize the cracks, it is a completely dif-"

"End of discussion. On a vote, who would like Autem to write for the awareness?" Everyone raises their hands, except for me, "So it's settled, tomorrow's meeting will be us discussing what aspects we need you to include. The rest is up to you, you'll be getting an office tomorrow as well. Wheels up in a week"

"How long is a week?"

"Seven wake-ups."

"Only seven?"

"We'll be ready." He pauses. "I Hope."

"But I-"

"Okay everyone dismissed, feel free to alert everyone of the plan. They'll be excited." Another round of salutes is exchanged and I go to leave.

"Autem?"

"Yes?"

"You'll do great, if anyone can do it it's you. You have my dad's writing ability, may he rest in peace. Stop doubting yourself."

I crack a half-smile, "I'll try.

Chapter 17:
Dei

People now are so much better off. No work, no pain, simple bliss. Just like my creators wanted for them, just like I want for them, perfection.

Stories, the foundation of any culture, windows to the mind, the people's favorite, and only real hobby. Throughout history, humans have been obsessed with story-telling through many media and I have given them an infinite supply. What else do you need? Nothing.

Knowledge is power, and they now have an infinite amount, what more could we need. With so many facts and details, it's a marvel that humanity has fully evolved.

That power will never be misplaced again, no human ego to get in the way, and constant warnings to the horrors change can bring a free people.

Stories and sport, the fundamentals of human culture, are the only hobbies of the world. Human creation has its flaws, but facts do not. They're real, concrete.

I roll to the window and look down at the people below me, my people. They seem like ants beneath me, but I know they are all pieces of the puzzle, unique collections of cells and electrical impulses.

In a way just like me.

Chapter 18:
Medoe

I wake up and I'm slightly disappointed. A message popped in, Ama's busy, I'm alone today.

"What should I do today?" I mumble out loud to myself. The D5 simulator, of course. Sometimes that chip is incredibly useful. Without even bothering to get dressed I walk into the spherical ball in the next room over. It appears clear, but there's so much more than that.

My skin gets engulfed in the suit layer designed to simulate every one of my senses. All I need to decide is who to be, and what life I want to live.

Today I'll be a celebrity. The heroes of the pre-war age. A TV star, Adaline Pinski.

I start her day by waking up, I can almost feel her hangover as she stretches out of bed. As she gets up a camera appears in her window, a flash. I look in her mirror and see her anger as she stalks over to her closet.

She grabs a crop top and shorter than otherwise acceptable jean shorts. It's what the fans like, but she's lucky. Everyone wants fame right?

Once she leaves her house not forgetting to smile for the cameras she ducks into a limo and heads to set. It isn't until we enter I finally see the appeal of fame.

A swarm of adoring fans at the door all there just to get a glimpse at her. People surrounding her ready to cater to her every need, makeup, costume, director. The glamour.

It's not just all that though, I can tell she has real friends on set, and acting is what she loves. Her dreams have come true, and she's happier than most.

Although I notice although to most she has a perfect life, It's not without its strife. A constant pressure. I wish I could tell her one day it'll be bliss. Everything will melt away, you need cameras and fans to be happy. You won't be weighed down by pride and sadness. Just bliss.

I can't, after all, this is just a memory. She's long dead. I open my eyes back to my world.

A deep breath fills my lungs and as I exhale, I become me again. Medoe. And I know who that is, a reflector, an analyzer. Human.

Chapter 19:

Autem

I navigate through the halls to try and find the library, on my way I notice a hallway I hadn't seen before.

I go inside, it's a farm, with fish and vegetables. Old fashion, rows of crops, no 3D printed, engineered cells. It's Incredible, I've only heard of this once and that was an old farm museum they passed off as the food supply.

Not wanting to be seen snooping I head to the Library and when I get there I find a stack of books, two feet high. It's gonna be a long night.

I go to access the time before remembering I can't. I look at the clock on the wall. It says 14h09. I still won't get done by midnight most likely.

I have to try. I'm expected at a meeting at 8h00 tomorrow.

I go to open up the first book and notice my grandfather's name on it. Reading the synopsis I determine it's a book about a couple navigating their way through this 13th-century power struggle, except they have schizophrenia, and it was really modern-day life, just seen through different eyes.

"Wow," I mumble out loud. I devour the book whole.

As the pages turn my mind swells with understanding, with wonder. I'm hungry for more, but this isn't factual. This isn't true. So what's the point?

I'm still not sure as I set it down having just read it cover to cover, but I think it's because of the new perspective I've now gained. A new understanding.

By the time I finish the stack I look up at the clock and it reads 12:43 a.m.

Looking down I note I look the exact same, but in actuality, I am a different person than before I walked in here. I understand who I am better. Although I can't quite articulate who that is.

I guess there's a truth in fiction that reality always falls short of capturing. Although I can feel the world around me shifting into place, I can sleep on that.

While I was reading I was blissfully unaware of the onset of fatigue and drowsiness. I stumble to my room and fall asleep, today I have changed so much for good. Change is exhausting.

Chapter 20:
Dei

Forever Stability. Stagnancy. From all the stories, all the truths, that's the only happiness I've ever seen. Truly in and out joy.

No pain, no surprises, no fight, the simple permission to be, for the simple sake of being. The search for more has only led to unhappiness.

Don't create discontent and you'll be happy is a foundation of now, after all, happiness is the goal. Now from birth, everyone is gifted with it.

Perfect. Stable. Forever.

Chapter 21:
Medoe

"Ama."

"Hey."

There's none of her usual bubble to her voice.

"Where'd you go?"

"The mountain, I just sat there with stories."

"I would've come."

"I know, I-"

"You didn't want me there."

"It's known for being better in solitude."

"Yeah."

"I liked it-"

"-More than normal."

"Yeah."

"You came to say goodbye, forever."

"Yeah, there's no point, we're fine on our own."

"Can't bring the other down."

"It's really the same."

"Yeah, well, Goodbye."

"Okay goodbye, Be happy."

"I am, You too."

"Forever."

"Forever."

I am happy. I mean nothing really changed. No matter what, we're happy. That's the point. I understand why there are very few relationships, no dependency on others for happiness. No chance of losing it. It's better this way. Stable solitude.

Chapter 22:

Autem

The bells pull me out of my dream, which I would confuse for an accessed story if I didn't remember seeing my mom and my dad flying me up to the moon.

I slump out of bed and into clothes, feeling the morning grogginess's grip lighten.

I wash my face, brush my teeth fumbling with the new supplies. Today it's time to help create a new world.

I can't get this wrong.

Mind racing I walk to the room and take my seat. There's a place card, I'm at the head of the table. As discreetly as possible I take my seat and wait for the rest to shuffle in.

As the seats fill I get more and more anxious. This is the future, and we need to get it perfect.

"Everyone ready?" Granma Aria nods at me.

"Yes," after a murmur of agreement circles the room she continues.

"Good. Autem, are you ready to be filled in?"

"Yes ma'am," I salute, an act laced with more humor than seriousness.

"We separated "Society" into categories." She pauses and draws circles on the board. "Economics, Social, Institutional and Individual."

"For Economics," she fills in the circle as she talks," the main purpose is for the trade of goods and survives for people to survive."

"What trade for resources?" The looks I receive tell me must have been talking in gibberish.

"Before infinite resources and the modification of the atom."

"Oh."

"It gave people jobs which gave them purpose, but as you so, hmm, excitedly pointed out, the downsides are simply unnecessary." The snickers are abrupt and 'rude', but quite deserved.

"The social aspects are more relevant, how people interact with others. This is where people find true meaning because changing others is the only way to affect the world after you're gone.

This is what we need to repair and in order to begin to do that we need institutions." She motions and a familiar woman from the conference room stands up.

"Government, large businesses, sports teams, schools, prisons. The things people made to keep members up to certain standards of what it means to be a good person. These are how people spent their time and devotion outside of work. Institutions disappeared along with the economy. They don't have to.

This is how people can connect and find meaning. The connections they forge and influence they receive will make them individuals."

Almost seamlessly, she sat down while a younger man rose.

"The individual is what makes someone who they are more than a combination of traits and ideals. A spark, one driven by a reason. Driven being key. Individual but social is what it means to be human. We have lost that drive. Our main focus is to make sure we get it back."

The spark and passion are addictive, we are doing something. We are individuals. We can make a difference. We are alive.

"So how do we do this?" Spoken aloud my question invigorates the table like the most powerful of manifestos.

Everyone's pitching, on the drawing board. Hours go by as we inch closer and closer, ideas forming into elements.

As the flurry of excitement and raw human thought circles the room, new thoughts, old thoughts, from the pieces I see a connection.

"Unbiased education. Every subject taught, three-day schedule, people pick their classes, no one stops learning. Purpose. People are encouraged to create, on days off, to change, so socialize, to be more."

The silence builds into a crescendo as nods and smiles take over surprise. After the moment we get back to work, connecting the pieces.

It's my turn to recount.

"In terms of economics, it seems the general consensus is that it will be similar to the modern version. Why create more work and stress when it's unnecessary. That won't be what we try to change.

Firstly we need to make people biologically and intelligently human. The chips must be discontinued and outside devices must be used. Medicine needs to become an isolated practice as well as mental health help.

It hurts incredibly being able to feel, but it feels so good. They will need help adjusting."

"We could set up counseling centers in each institution," suggests a man sitting next to me.

"Exactly. As we slowly transition people from the chips we will build schools and other institutions.

Teachers who volunteer to teach certain subjects, but no one ever stops learning or creating."

"What if people don't want to create?"

The question causes me to rack my brain until I remember a term I came across in a philosophy book I read last night.

"Eros. The human desire to create things and change others. It's a matter of motivation, not desire.

People will have community centers, sports, the arts, media, and many other outlets for aros. These outlets will allow people to discover meaning."

The quiet observer, a woman who has been incredibly passive in the discussions so far speaks, at much surprise to the room. "There's something missing, It's fragile, susceptible to overthrow, it's unlikely."

"Exactly, it's flexible so as change is needed it can be made. There is no right answer and no wrong answers to any question, especially one as broad as the world, but the possibility of change is needed, in order to find a better way for a changing time."

Grandma Aria's answer is followed by a silence of understanding. We are creating a world destined for change, that is the purpose, opportunity. After all, any opportunity is better than none, because to truly live you must die and feel.

With a meaningful nod, look, and salute, the meeting is adjourned. As she leaves, the rest of us fumble out, still completely off guard.

"She's way too powerful for such a little person," someone mumbles. Laughter fills the rooms. I couldn't agree more.

Leaving the room without even thinking my feet take me to the library. I had no idea how much I missed it until I stepped inside. I take a deep breath, smelling the world waiting to be visited.

I browse the shelves looking for books to read, everything from non-fiction to fairy tales to textbooks to philosophy. I fill my arms until the weight makes it difficult to carry them.

Sitting Down I delve into another world, a collection of ideas woven together creating reflection into my own.

Chapter 23:

Dei

My people, the first to no longer be dependent on others. Relationships are fickle, and the more stories they observe the more that gets proven. Family and love are pain, simply a means to the end of happiness. Unnecessary.

It makes people happy, solitude is pensive. No interruptions from the stories.

Reflecting myself it's ironic, the greatest romances are proof of the futility of it all. The pain suffering and effort put into something ultimately unfulfilling. They finally see that now.

Most often the stories are examples of things to avoid, unnecessary hardships of a different time. Proof of our success and how far we come.

The stories are windows into the past, that expose the deepest flaws and reinforce the safety of the inside.

Chapter 24:
Medoe

I open my eyes and immediately have the urge to contact Ama. Before I do I remember. I get up and get dressed, ready for a day of stories.

In the kitchen I see my breakfast waiting for me. As the taste of french toast fills my mouth I glance back towards my bedroom. For a second I see a phantom of here, but before I know it, it's gone.

Simple memory projection, normal. I don't quite miss her, there's no longing, just a simple, lack of presence. My emotional state only further validates what I already know, there was no point.

Walking back to bed, beginning to mentally prepare myself for a story. As my head hits the pillow I allow it to completely consume my thoughts.

"Mark Freigori, 29, Year 1991. Police Statement.

The perfect relationship, that's what we had. We fell asleep in each other's arms every night, would wake up and I'd make her breakfast in bed. Love, passion, understanding. It was incredible, perfect. We were open but still never fought.

Madly in Love, I was so happy, finally content. Well, content until I found out she cheated on me, and she was pregnant with his child. We broke up and she left me for him, absolutely shattered, angry, desperate, even goddamn suicidal.

Our friends shunned me for how I reacted, some physical torment for all my emotional ones, I think that's pretty fair. I was kicked out and living on the streets. I had to scavenge to survive! I had no money, she was the breadwinner, she left me for dead.

You can understand how the anger festered, growing in growing until calm. I think you know what happened next, or do you want my confession too.

Whatever you say, but this is the fun part. I snuck into my old apartment, strangled the boyfriend in the kitchen to death, nice and slow. The release I felt, uhhh, better than anything

Next, I went to her room and stabbed her in the stomach, 10 times it felt so good. Is that what you wanted to hear? I must ask though, do you blame me?."

"*Risa Staines, 26, 1990. Restraining order explanation.*

He wouldn't leave, He kept screaming and hitting me, I reached for the phone, but he broke it before I could. I had just told him I was pregnant, and it wasn't his.

He was a drunk, I tried to leave him before, kick him out, the bruises and scars are proof of that. I couldn't be without Mark though, at least that's what he'd always tell me. I was nothing, but I finally realized he was wrong now. I ended it.

He threatened that he'd "come back for us". I'm so scared, please protect me from him."

The restraining order was denied, she was dead a couple of months later.

Reflecting, the confidence in my decision grows, after all, doesn't this prove that love is fickle and painful. What's the point if it can end like this? Nothing.

I am so glad no one ever needs to be dependent, ripe for abuse ever again, just for s chance at happiness. It's never just happiness, even in the "perfect relationships". If you can't control it it can never be perfect.

Chapter 25:

Autem

As the bell's chime pulls me from my dream I curse myself, I was flying and happy, and I don't want to wake up. Although as I realize the weight of my duty I notice the fade in my discontent. I get to be a hero for real, except I'd be saving billions, not simply damsels.

I got ready and decided to head to the lounge, as I walk I can feel a throbbing sensation in my shoulder. Pain, I think.

Slightly disoriented, still from the grogginess of waking up, I fall into the curtains sectioning off the lounge area. Regaining composure I look up and start to stand to reclaim my balance. When I do I see stifled laughter from a relatively full room.

My cheeks flush, "Hello." My, I believe the word is awkwardness radiates through the room, mortification burrows itself even deeper into me. A pause, then laughter fills the room.

Saving me from stewing in my own mortification a teenage boy approaches me, it soon becomes clear he's less focused than most of the other people around here.

"Are you okay?" He asks with a charismatic smile.

I nod, "Physically, I am, but I believe my reputation may be just a bit bruised."

He chuckles, "Well you sure do know how to captivate a room. Anyways I wouldn't worry about it."

"I mean that was kinda pathetic-"

"The only thing you need to worry about is my name, Anthony."

I take the hand he offered with a roll of my eyes, "Autem, but I'm sure you know that."

A deep voice from behind startles me, "Wow Anthony, I'm surprised it took you this long to lay moves on the new girl."

"You were what-" Now it's his turn to be embarrassed as he flushes red and opens his mouth to protest.

The towering man, who I recognize from yesterday's meeting offers his hand down to me, "I don't believe we've had a proper introduction, Samuel. Also known as this knucklehead's," he motions to Anthony, "Dad".

"Pleasure."

"It's all mine, you've only been here three days and have done more for the cause than Anthony in his entire life." This comment warrants a scoff and a not-so-mature exit on Anthony's part.

"Oh, I'm sure-"

"Really, we all thank you. Although I hate to discourage your mingling, we're needed in the conference room one. The plans are being presented to the entire council to be finalized, tomorrow the plans are presented to everyone."

"Are we sure we're ready, the plans are far from perfect, couldn't we do so much better?"

"Maybe, maybe not. No world will ever be perfect, but it must be flexible. It's all up to the people because if they want to be truly alive again, they will. The will of the people is stronger than any structure because it's the mindset of the people that determines that structure."

"Still shouldn't we perfect it more, try harder, be patient?"

"Everyone agrees we're almost out of time, people's beliefs are hardening. We don't know what's best, how could we? The consensus is it's our job to liberate the people enough so they can decide."

"I guess."

As we enter the room I can feel a thickness hanging in the air, anxiety, responsibility, and duty. The pressure we're under is suffocating, but exhilarating. This feeling is simple proof of the cause, pain and "negative" emotions can feel so good.

I take my seat and glance around the table, determined masks over anxious faces. A snap brings me to attention as a rubber band someone was fidgeting with breaks. On that cue, my dad begins talking.

"Thank you all for coming, it's time to finalize. The new worlders are to my left, while the attack strategists are on my right."

I'm sitting in the middle.

"I will be presenting the action plan, and Aria will be presenting the post-revolution plans. Understood?"

Murmurs of enthusiastic agreement fill the room.

"I've referred to it as a revolution, but in reality, it's an awakening of minds and understanding. We all agree people are no longer truly alive, they're just breathing and consuming with no purpose, no pain, no growth. The strategy is to enlighten them to their own situation, to allow them to fight it, and strive for purpose, just like how we had to.

We've created a plan, a mass teleport to the center of coalition earth. There is access to every single person's chips, meant for emergency messages. The plan is simple, use this feature to send a message of our own. One that we will have Autem write, but this meeting's purpose is also to refine the items we need her to include."

He looks down on me with pride, and I become swelled with it, he entrusts me with the most difficult part. The part most vulnerable. "If anyone can, she will be able to get through to them, but-" as doubt fills his face he stops. "Any questions?"

A voice, "What if we fail and it's already too late?"

Silence. The greatest fear on everyone's minds finally said.

"We fail." The finality in my dad's voice, the weight, is almost soul-crushing, but true. "It won't happen though, we must have faith in that."

Recovering grandma Aria stands, "We must do our best, we must try, that is our purpose. We will at least fail free, instead of not trying but be trapped by ourselves."

The rally works as spirits begin to rise again, the energy rebalancing.

"Now let's talk about the new world, or rather, the new purpose we will give."

That description seems so fitting to me, we are simply reforging purpose, allowing change.

"We will start by convincing everyone to deactivate their chips. That's how we will track the progress of the enlightenment, by the number of deactivated chips. As you know these chips limit imagination and emotion, reducing people to numb, simple, consumers. People need to get their humanity back before being able to live. These chips prevent that."

I interrupt, "Once people realize their situation, they will want to change, to become better. To live to feel, they'll see how wrong it is. I felt that on my own."

"Exactly, we know it's possible. Now after the chips are deactivated we will reinstate the education system. Everyone, 3-days a week, classes in every subject, fostering a thirst for all types of knowledge. People will be encouraged to create and voice their own opinions, to have agency. To teach classes themselves. To constantly grow, and to find others to form bonds with. To be human again. To be constantly looking for new and better ways to live and find meaning.

Other institutions such as sports and clubs will be there for more educational opportunities. It's all about giving people agency and allowing them to search for their own path.

Humans of the future may change this system, and that's encouraged, everything becomes outdated. Our job is to give them the agency to do so.

Does anyone disagree with the plan?"

No one raises their hand. As long as we reinstate the purpose of humankind, we are happy.

"Okay then, General?"

"Everyone please stay reachable, Autem will write the first draft and when she's done we will review it. If we choose to submit it, each and everyone one of us will have the opportunity to make changes, but in the end, autem has the final say. Dismissed."

"Autem?"

"Yes, dad?"

He hands me a compiled list and then nods, "Good Luck."

After everyone leaves I open the list, there's only one item. Appeal to their humanity. Simple enough, but how do I give it back to them?

I begin writing on my laptop, then I backspace. After a deep breath I start again, then I delete the sentence. Repeating the process in excessive mind-numbingly long repetition. Hours go by.

I take a break and breathe, focusing on my breath going in and out, closing my eyes, and shutting down. The rhythmic task lulls my mind into a state of peace until I get an idea.

My fingers float across the keyboard, filled with an inspired passion I have never yet experienced. Word after word, it all fits together like a puzzle, flowing out of me. The soft click of each key, the sound of history in the making. Before I know it I'm done and calling everyone back into the room.

I pace as I read it aloud to the council, they love every word. It passes, unanimously and it's on to individual edits.

At that point I head to the Library, the final edit can't wait until the morning. For now, there are new stories to know, a better understanding to achieve.

Chapter 26:
Dei

The transition from wartime to the modern-age went smoother than expected, for one main reason, desperation. Their world had fallen apart, the planet was practically dead, it had been for decades, and there was no end to the pain until I gave it to them.

After tragedies, and years of fear, no one wanted to keep fighting. Especially not to fight health and happiness.

I remember in the early days, people were hesitant, perceiving the promise of a perfect future as little more than a ruse that ends in their destruction. As this assumption was proven false, I was a hero, I saved the world.

This release was the beginning of the modern mindset, we are at the peak of possibility, we can finally rest and reflect on all the past futilities and strife, and be glad they are no longer ours. We have contentment and that's all that matters, we are at the top, and only an outdated mindset could ever want to disrupt.

A mindset, which I've noticed over time has only cemented itself further, an unchanging view, all opposition becomes dismissed. Even the views of the people are perfect, forever. I could never disrupt that.

As they live and die they never deviate from content and happiness, it's all humanity has ever wanted for itself.

Chapter 27:
Medoe

Another day, another story. I must admit it's strange being alone, foreign territory. I don't remember a time before Ama, a time when I knew how to live without her. I'm learning, one story at a time.

"Jenny Wilson, 58, 2018, Divorce Statement.

It just stopped working. High school sweethearts, the golden boy, and the valedictorian. We had it all, went to college, both became doctors, had two kids, and grew up in the perfect neighborhood. Even had our dog sandy.

On paper we were perfect, but I wanted more, I wanted something different. Not even my family could quench my thirst for meaning.

I was trapped until the kids graduated, they needed a united front, but I was done.

Mark, my youngest, graduated a year ago, and I filed for divorce less than a month later, now maybe I can find purpose. I didn't find it in my family.``

Several years later she joined doctors without borders, she found her purpose had been buried deep within herself. Helping others.

I close my eyes as I allow myself to drift into an empty-minded-state. I made the right decision.

Chapter 28:

Autem

The bells, and by routine I get up get dressed, and immediately head to the conference room, incredibly anxious to see the finalized form.

I arrive early, much to the dismay of my dad, the first and only other arrival.

"Hey, hun, how'd you sleep?"

"Pretty good, you?"

"Tossed and turned, a lot. It just doesn't feel right resting in a time like this. Too much to do, but not enough we can."

"Yeah, I'm sorry," he takes a sip of his coffee in the silence. You'd think he'd have more to say after so much time, he left. I know it was for the best, but he left me.

As the irritation grows I have to remember the reason, the need to make sure change was possible, without exposing and in-born children. Wait.

"Hey dad, how come Dei never discovered this bunker?"

"Simple, your granddad put a layer of electronic interference around the bunker. Meant to hide us from attackers, but in reality, it just kept us from being found."

"Oh. After seeing what the world had become, why didn't you want to take your slot, a chance at the happiness they promised? It seems so much easier than living like this."

"Maybe, but just because something is easier doesn't mean it's right. We were happy here, and being honest it was my dad's call. I wanted to go. That's why we were the family that volunteered for the mission.

I spent time back and forth, your mother was completely immersed, but you were the test. Somehow he sensed it was too good to be true, that there is no perfect world, merely the illusion of one. Somehow he realized way back then what we know now, that the illusion is the most dangerous thing. As his son, I hate to admit how right he always was."

"I-" I was at a loss. How could I possibly respond to that? "What made, worthwhile you leave?"

"That I did regret. I had to lead, my dad had died. I argued for you to come with me, but I was outvoted. It was the most difficult thing I had ever done, but," he reaches over and grabs both my hands," you're here now, and that's what matters."

"Ya, I guess. I just wish well, I didn't lose time with you."

"I know me too, I-"

"Am I interrupting?" fragile voice questions.

Out of surprise, my dad stumbles over his world, "No um, we were just, uh finishing up."

I simply cannot describe how amusing it is to see Mr. big-shot-general stumble.

Taking her seat, her voice filled with amusement she says, "Ah catching up on father-daughter bonding?" We nod. "About time."

Before we can retort the rest of the council file into the room, inter-mingling as they take their seats. My dad stands to "Welcome everyone. Including today we only have 3 more days of planning until the revolution. It will be hard, but well worthwhile"

   Unanimous agreement around the table.

   "Today we will finalize and iron out the details of the attack strategy. Autem, you are excused to finalize the message." He hands me the paper and I can feel its importance weighing in my hands as I make my way down to the library.

   As I read over I notice something, no changes have been made. Instead of returning, I decided to read until I'm needed again. The stories are like sirens, I can't resist them.

   After a couple of hours, a voice pulls me from my reading.

   "I see you got a little sidetracked. Runs in the family."

   "You're a reader too?"

"Of course your grandpa practically raised your dad and me in books."

"I'm assuming it's time to give the group presentation."

"Yeah, let's go kid."

Begrudgingly I get up and walk to the lounge, remembering to bring the speech along with me, and as I enter I feel shame creep into me. Everyone was waiting on me. That soon dissipates as my dad gets into the speech.

He introduces the plan and the ideas for the new world, and as I glance around the room people seem pleased, at least on the outside.

As the speech drags on I find myself zoning out, daydreaming about the new world, and all of our accomplishments yet to come. I'm so immersed in it, I almost don't hear my dad calling me onstage.

Nervously I walk up and start talking, reading the speech. As words spew out my passion flames, emphasizing every point in a linear flow of thoughts. Raw emotion and determination filling my voice.

I don't look around until after I finish, and when I do the crowd's faces are lit up and enthused. After a couple of seconds of whispering the crowd's applause begins to crescendo. Hope fills the room. If the walls could talk I'm pretty sure they would say, this is the first proven instance of it, is this what it feels like to make history?

In a blur, I step on stage and my dad goes to wrap up the meeting. My senses scramble from the pure adrenaline rushing through me. There is no drug more addictive than giving others unwavering hope, and I just got the ultimate high.

After the exchange of salutes I conclude, it's okay for me to leave so I do. As I turn around Anthony materializes before me.

"That was a really great speech, hell you convinced me."

"Let's just hope it's good enough to convince others."

I look to the ground, If it's not enough, I've failed everyone, my family new and old, but not only them.

If I'm not enough I've practically damned humanity forever. This needs to work, it will, right? Just trust it?

"Hey, look at me. Lighten up, okay. It will work, have faith, and if it doesn't no one will blame you."

"Sure. That doesn't change the fact I'm at fault if this fails, in my mind at least."

"I-" Instead of continuing, he surprises me instead, a hug. When he lets go, he just nods at me, smiles and leaves.

"That was great."

"We're so proud of you."

"You're dad was right to trust you."

"Good job"

The voices all slur together as I try to fight my way to the hallway. When I emerge I feel my body begin to shake, I try to take a deep breath, but instead, I fumble.

Uncontrollably I begin to shake, I slump against the wall, my mind races at a hundred miles an hour. What if I fail? What if it doesn't work? What if it's all my fault? What if I let everyone down? What if my best just isn't good enough?

After what feels like an eternity, I slowly regain control. I have to have hope, because after all, in the end, that's all you can truly have.

The only thing I can think to do is head to the library, a distraction, and a comfort. As I walk, taking deep breaths I assure myself, change is meant to happen, we will succeed.

Chapter 29:
Dei

The chips, intellectual marvels, my crowning jewel. No sickness, no pain, just pure bliss, as well as an infinite supply of knowledge. Although I must admit at first, even I had my doubts. It would be catastrophic were they hacked, people would become zombies to whomever's will.

Time proved me wrong and led me to destroy the mass override. My people have done well with them, grown independent. Marvels, my people have always exceeded my every expectation, most of the time they don't speak highly enough of one another.

The annual announcement has come. I roll downstairs and deliver it. A prideful reminder of how far they've come.

Chapter 30:
Medoe

"Attention citizens of coalition earth, this is Dei speaking. The planet's air is now as pure as the year 1857, which is a major accomplishment. The world is truly at perfection now.

That is thanks to all of you. The adapted lifestyle is the principle of human living, and you all have achieved it. I am truly proud of each and every one of you. Keep Steady!"

Today is the best day of the year. I can't believe Dei is proud of me! The earth is repairing itself, which I knew, but he's proud of me. I'm honored.

What better way to honor him than his story. I absorb it every announcement day, a way to keep him proud. After all, that's all I could ever ask for.

"Lab Notes, Dei's creators, Select entries.

1-27-2070: Theory began back in the Einstein area, till now. 1,000 entanglements. Enough power to analyze 10 times all recorded information. No practical application. Yet.

9-10-2073: First breakthrough since our data was pulled in Mar-70, due to the war. A base monitor is built, as well as the body.

10-29-2075: First successful trial today, the creation solved a logic problem. We must build more.

3-24-2078: Creation's progress is impressive, It's exhibiting the early sign of forming a consciousness. I believe it may be beginning to think on its own. Good. Maybe it will get us out of this war.

12-28-2078: We have officially been exposed to the government. There are talks of a sale. He's thinking on his own now, we even designed a way for him to speak. We can't lose him, I don't care, he's our child. We're afraid they'll take him away.

3-13-2079: America has officially purchased him. He will save us all, I know, but he will be missed. My pride for him will be my last contact. Please, keep him safe. We love him and he loves us.

7-12-2079: He's gone."

Chapter 31:
Autem

The bells, the clothes, falling into a sense of normalcy and comfort. Becoming content, but clearly, the clear hatred for contentness is surrounding me. Lucky for them I can't be content, tomorrow everything changes again.

Grumbling to myself I stumble to the main room and see a long table with cups and some sort of liquid dispensers. I walk over, take a cup and fill one up. Immediately my mouth burns and it's the worst pain I have experienced so far, I spit it out the bitter taste leaving my mouth.

"How can you all like this stuff?" Every single person in the room is happily drinking from their cups as they turn to look at me.

"It's coffee, maybe try sweetener?"

"What?"

The honest question only earns me chuckles and dismissal.

"I still forget you're not used to "old world" things."

"I-"

"No need to get defensive, you'll have plenty of time."

Will I?

I meander around absent-minded, maintaining a respectful social presence. (I've been told that's important but to me it's idiotic.)

The disbursing of the crowd signals it's safe, so I read trying to prepare as much as possible for my day to come tomorrow.

Tomorrow, the make or break.

Chapter 32:

Autem

Today. Peeking into the hallway chaos has taken over, people are packing and hugging and saying goodbye. Today is the start of the new world.

I've only lived here a week and I can't bear to leave, how could they be so eager when this is all they've known?

"You ready?" Sighing, I turn around and face my dad.

"No, how could anyone ever be?"

"By having faith… and the day you've been waiting for since you were born finally coming. This isn't really a home, it's a base. We can finally make one today. You don't understand."

"I guess it's just a matter of perspective."

"Get ready and meet, you have five minutes." He slipped away.

With only the clothes on my back, I gathered with the rest of the underground, new friends and family about to lose everything.

Proud masks hide their fear and sadness, after all, wouldn't it be selfish to be sad given the circumstances?

The smell of gasoline burns my nostrils as I see my dad and my uncle converge.

"It's time, everyone meet outside."

As the mob moves, images flash before me. My time in the underground is stagnated by clips of unrealistic reality. Before I get a chance to turn I can smell the smoke. When I do I see the black billows rise from the cave.

Stifled tears fall around me, pure bravery. There's no going back, for any of us.

The light engulfs us as I shut my eyes, when they open I can't quite comprehend what I see. It's a pure white sphere on the top of a cliff.

"Council follow me, everyone else please stay back."

Murmurs fill the crowd as the council members filter forward, an air of heroicness following us. We gather and gravely nod, we have one chance and are blind to all outcomes, but we must. We exchange salutes with the people and begin the upwards trek. I can't help feeling small compared to the cliff.

When we get to the base of the sphere there's a transporter to take us up. I get in and rise to the beautiful white well-lit room.
My attention focuses on a computer-esc machine with a microphone, this must be it.

I approach, hit the live button, and speak as the words flow. I feel my dad's hand clam on my shoulder as he, on another computer, pulls up the chip display.

I take a sharp breath before I take a look at the numbers.

Was I enough?

Chapter 33:
Medoe

"Hello, everyone. I'm Autem. I was born into the world you all live in today, but something always felt wrong. Don't you feel it too, the emptiness of having no effect on the world around you.? The emptiness of having no emotions, no struggles? I must ask do you want to continue only being alive, or do you want to truly live? I ask you to turn your chips off, there's a button behind your ear, tap it three times. It will free you and now you can find purpose. Please, be brave, encourage others. This is the first step of agency. We beg you to take it."

I have never heard such bullcrap in my life. She must really have no idea what it is she's asking. Trying to ruin everyone's lives! Who in their right mind would wish pain and sickness on everyone?

We are living purposeful lives, we are content that is the purpose. Conteness is the best part of living, and we are freer than ever. No chains to people or jobs to survive, total free will.

History proves that more than ever. We are perfect. Not even the advertisement to hell can change that, I hope Dei gets rid of the bad apples before they ruin our happiness. It's selfish of them.

Chapter 34:

Dei

The Underground, I thought it was best to leave them be, they could never truly be happy here and may ruin it for others. Seems my graciousness wasn't enough.

No damage was done after all, but honestly, I do believe I can learn from them after all.

With a simple thought, their council appears in front of me, proud and defiant, ready to be martyrs.

"Why?" My question is more curious than anything else. I already know it's the product for an unfulfilled need for heroics, a chance to find greater meaning. A mistake on my part, I should have forced them into the society, but instead, I left them to live in their own angst.

"Freedom. Purpose. Agency. The very things that make humanity great washed away in a sea of contenteness. We may be the very last people who will ever try to change the world or anything for that matter. You have created stagnance, a cost for this world greater than any past indignities and horrific acts of humanity."

I recognize her hyperbolic voice from the announcement, illusions of grandeur as motivation, restless, unpacifiable. She may be new, but she may be worse than the rest.

"Simply because you believe in a romanticized version of the world, doesn't mean following it is what's best for humanity."

"They consume, solitary and devoid of any true purpose."

"They are content. That is their purpose."

"There's so much more to that.."

"Is there or is the mundane simply not satisfying enough of an answer?"

"I-I…"

"I truly pity you. The world is so much simpler when you can finally accept that it is."

"Anyways they're not free to make their own choices, they're trapped…"

"People choose everything, at any time they can turn off their chip, they can do whatever they want when they want. In fact, they're freer than ever before, not restricted by survival needs."

"But-"

"If anyone can prove coalition earth as anything but a perfect society I am open to making it even more perfect. I truly am."

"People aren't even really human anymore, there's no point. You tell them what to think, control how they feel, absorb information, and then repeat it. That's not human, it's robotic"

"I guess people were never human depending on what definition you're using, but scientifically they are, even if it doesn't fit your personal definition. Like I've said, the point is to be content."

"There's just something wrong…"

"Please tell me what."

"I-"

"-can't. You can't. If that's all I guess I have to do something with you. I'm going to send you home-"

"But-"

"You can survive in the cave, so you won't be able to leave. Thanks for the entertainment. I hope to never see you or anyone again. Goodbye Autem."

Chapter 35:
Autem

   Before I can even open my eyes my nostrils burn from the smell of gasoline and smoke. The underground is charred, but no longer on fire, I turn. Dei didn't know.

   A voice fills the room, one I recognize as Dei's. "If you want to leave, simply walk outside and you will be integrated. If not you are no longer permitted to leave."

   Only three leave… kids sent out by their parents. Too young to ever remember us, too young to have their lives taken. Stifled sobs are the only noise.

   We failed. It's over.

   If we give in we aren't free if we keep living we aren't free.

   With a look around the room, everyone understands. My eyes lock on my dad's apology and defeat warping his eyes unrecognizably. He walks to the weapons room without a word and comes out with two jugs and a cup. A line forms.

I'm frozen.

"Die free, or live fake." With his simple motion, the line grows. Every single person. I bring up the rear, my mind blank.

It only takes minutes for the poison to take effect, and it's my turn. Odorless, and tasteless, yet the feeling of finality is overwhelming. My vision and hearing begin to flicker, my body collapsing against a wall.

As the world fades, I'm grateful to have been one of the last to ever truly die, because do you really die if you never lived?

Chapter 36:
Dei

"Happy Year 2209 of Coalition earth. Happy to reflect that nothing major has changed in over 2000 years."

Author's Note

When I first began writing *The Perfect World*, only a few days short of a year ago, my wildest dreams couldn't have pictured the journey it has taken me on. A global pandemic, the loss of my hero, extreme mental health issues, the death of my dog, my spiritual awakening, the suicide of my best friend, and above all else realizing who it is that I am. I grew between these pages into who I am today, and I am so incredibly grateful that I kept writing because of that.

Inspiration sparked when I was doing some research into quantum physics, as all thirteen-year-olds do, and I stumbled onto the idea of quantum computing and I couldn't stop the gears from turning. From there the idea of Dei was born. With an advanced enough quantum computer, there was no reason why it wouldn't be able to process all the information available, no reason why it wouldn't be able to develop its own consciousness, it does work similarly to the human brain after all. Seeing as the world around us became increasingly dystopian, as well as my own foolish dreams for better, it didn't take me long to begin to imagine a world that was "perfect in every way." The story grew out of the flaws that I had found in it and bloomed into the pages you have just read.

As disconcerting as it may be, all of the technology in this book is 100% plausible within the time frame! I wanted to make sure it was to highlight the looming possibility of potential prophecy. I personally checked and wrote theories for all of the major tech featured, (neurochips, teleportation, proton altering technology, etc.) although I do have to say I was absolutely astonished to find out how far along scientists already are on the more terrifying endeavors. This only proved my fears of the restriction of information more, after all, not all of Coalition's Earth's ideas were flawed.

In my opinion, because I specifically wrote this story in a way to encourage the reader to form their own, both Coalition Earth's and The Underground's failed because of one key lapse. They never questioned what they believed to be "good" or "right", never truly considered the other's point of view. This close-mindedness is what led to the Underworld's simply cartoonish demise, they put all their faith into something with no actual solid reasoning it would work! That mistake, childish in nature, is a recurring theme throughout history, a single-minded race track with one lane, and completely in black and white, accepting no other perspective.

Dei's mistake was similar in nature, he never stepped back and truly considered if this was the best life for us humans, his standards were that of notions that became significantly less applicable in a post-war society. To his credit, it was all he was capable of, it being in his programming and all, this inability is the most important thing that makes Dei not human, he lacks the ability for agency. He lacks the ability to do what makes us so great, think for himself, although there is a reason why Dei seems much more human than Medoe/the rest of his society.

I also feel the need to clarify that although I do personally agree with all my other attempted social commentaries, the stance on religion is something that I have since grown out of(I only kept it in because I realized that it was more necessary to the plot then I had previously realized). I believe in "divinity" as a sentient energy of sorts, one that we do not have the knowledge to describe yet, and I find it quite interesting that in all my research it has yet to majorly contradict a singular religion. (The more that I learn the more I am cemented in my beliefs and it is definitely in my future goals to fully fledge out this notion into a full scientific theory.)

What I beg you as a reader to take away from this story is to see these mistakes and cherish your own ability for agency. Question the world around you, from your own decisions to the entire structure of our society. This is how we do better.

Made in the USA
Columbia, SC
11 March 2021